I Don't Like Peas

Written by
Marie Vinje

Illustrated by
Robin Michal Koontz

I don't like peas!

I won't eat peas!

Peas are mushy,
and they taste bad.

They slide off my fork,
which makes me mad.

5

They scoot off my plate
and onto the floor.

They roll all over,
even under the door.

Our cat likes peas.
She thinks peas are fun.

When a pea hits the floor,
she starts to run.

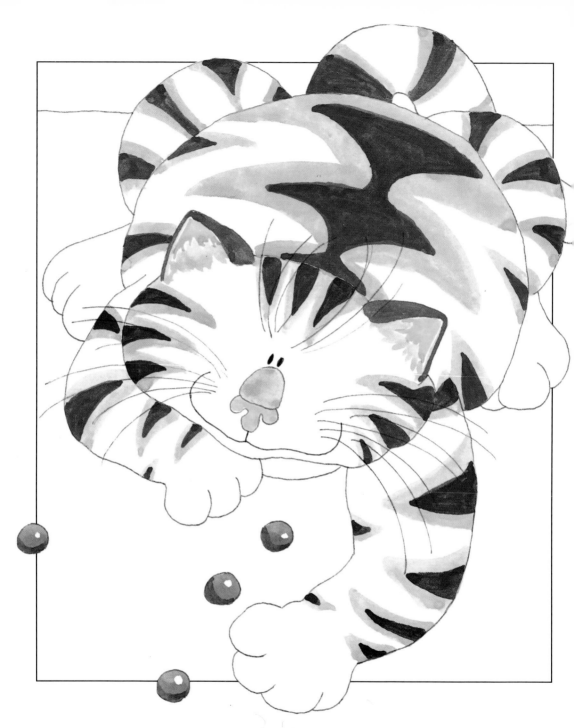

The cat thinks chasing
peas is a game.

If I could do that,
I'd think the same.

Maybe that's
what I should do.

I'll play a game
with peas, too.

The cat likes it better
when two of us play.

Now I want peas
every day!

Oops!